ELEMENTARY TREATISE ON
PARTIAL DIFFERENTIAL EQUATIONS

MAXWELL PRESS

ELEMENTARY TREATISE ON
PARTIAL DIFFERENTIAL EQUATIONS

George Biddell Airy K.C.B., M.A., LL.D., D.C.L

Astronomer Royal, Formerly Fellow of Trinity College
and
Lucasian Professor, Subsequently Plumian Professor of
Astronomy and Experimental Philosophy in the
University of Cambridge

MAXWELL PRESS

Chennai   Trichy   New Delhi

MAXWELL PRESS

This edition has been published in india by arrangement with Carson Books, UK

ISBN 978-93-91270-31-5   Maxwell Press

All rights reserved   No. 44, Nallathambi Street,
Printed and bound in India   Triplicane, Chennai 600 005

MJP 1145   © Publishers, 2023

Publisher :   C. Janarthanan

Publisher's Note

The legacy of a country is in its varied cultural heritage, historical literature, developments in the field of economy and science. The top nations in the world are competing in the field of science, economy and literature. This vast legacy has to be conserved and documented so that it can be bestowed to the future generation. The knowledge of this legacy is slowly getting perished in the present generation due to lack of documentation.

Keeping this in mind, the concern with retrospective acquiring of rare books has been accented recently by the burgeoning reprint industry. Maxwell Press is gratified to retrieve the rare collections with a view to bring back those books that were landmarks in their time.

In this effort, a series of rare books would be republished under the banner, "Maxwell Press". The books in the reprint series have been carefully selected for their contemporary usefulness as well as their historical importance within the intellectual. We reconstruct the book with slight enhancements made for better presentation, without affecting the contents of the original edition.

Most of the works selected for republishing covers a huge range of subjects, from history to anthropology. We believe this reprint edition will be a service to the numerous researchers and practitioners active in this fascinating field.

We allow readers to experience the wonder of peering into a scholarly work of the highest order and seminal significance.

MAXWELL PRESS

PREFACE TO THE FIRST EDITION.

THE work now offered to the University is strictly an Elementary Treatise. No attempt has been made to go into all the varied details, of methods and examples, which present themselves in the wide field of Partial Differential Equations, considered purely as an Algebraical subject.

I have endeavoured, however, to omit no important consideration affecting the Principles of those Equations. And I trust that the methods of solution here explained, and the instances exhibited, will be found sufficient for application to nearly all those important problems of Physical Science, which require for their complete investigation the aid of Partial Differential Equations.

G. B. AIRY.

ROYAL OBSERVATORY, GREENWICH,
 1866, *August* 15.

PREFACE TO THE SECOND EDITION.

SEVERAL verbal alterations are made in this Edition; two small paragraphs are added; and some sentences are introduced, referring to works in which examples of the application of the Theory of Partial Differential Equations may be found. But nothing is changed in the plan of the work, and no alterations are made in the numbering of the Articles.

G. B. AIRY.

ROYAL OBSERVATORY, GREENWICH,
1873, *July* 15.

INDEX.

ON PARTIAL DIFFERENTIAL EQUATIONS.

PRELIMINARY NOTICE ON INTEGRATION.

1. IN all that follows, we shall suppose that it is always possible to effect simple integration; inasmuch as any difficulties of integration, connected with the solutions of Partial Differential Equations, do not affect the principle of those solutions. Thus, for instance, we shall not hesitate to represent an unknown function of x by $\chi''(x)$, (the second differential-coefficient of $\chi(x)$), on the assumption that, whatever be the form of $\chi''(x)$, we can in some way find the function $\chi(x)$ of which it is the second differential-coefficient.

CHARACTERISTICS OF THE SOLUTIONS OF SIMPLE DIFFERENTIAL EQUATIONS.

2. Before entering on the subject of Partial Differential Equations, it may be convenient to consider some of the characteristics of the solutions of Simple Differential Equations.

3. To begin with Simple Differential Equations of the first order. Suppose, for facility of geometrical illustration, we consider the equation $y\dfrac{dy}{dx} = a$, or the equation

$y \dfrac{dx}{dy} = b$, of which the former, translated geometrically, indicates that the subnormal of a plane-curve (to be found) is constant, and the latter indicates that the subtangent is constant. The algebraical solutions are easily found: in each, there is a constant, which does not occur in the original differential equation, and is not defined by it; a constant of that class described (perhaps improperly) by the term "arbitrary," but which really means "not yet determined, but enabling us by proper determination of its value so to fix the value of x corresponding to a given value of y that we can adjust the solution to some specific condition."

The reader is requested to observe that instead of the term "arbitrary constant," we shall always use the term "undetermined constant."

4. If we treat the geometrical translation of the differential equation by a geometrical process, always drawing a normal or a tangent (as the case may be) so as to make the subnormal or subtangent constant, then drawing by means of it a small portion of the curve, then repeating the process, &c., we may produce a polygon which will approach to the strict solution, with smaller errors (by taking the sides small enough) than any small quantity that can be assigned. In each case, however, a starting-point is necessary.

5. In both ways (the algebraical and the geometrical) of treating the problems these conditions manifestly hold :—

The curve, in each case, is one definite curve.

The curve, in each case, is a continuous curve, expressed by the same equation through its whole extent.

Even if there be isolated points or curves, still the same one equation defines the whole.

It is necessary to introduce one undetermined quantity, enabling us to adjust the curve to a specific condition given by special considerations: that undetermined quantity is however a simple constant.

6. Let us now consider a Simple Differential Equation of the second order: such, for instance, as is given by this problem, " To find the curve in which the radius of curvature is a function, given in form, of the ordinate." Here the algebraic solution gives a formula requiring two undetermined quantities, still simple constants: the equivalent geometrical treatment shews that we require two elements (as, for instance, the value of x and the inclination of the tangent, for some one value of y). But all the conditions hold which are mentioned in Article 5: the only difference being that, instead of *one* undetermined quantity, a simple constant, there must now be *two* undetermined quantities, simple constants.

7. The conditions which will be found to hold in the solutions of Partial Differential Equations differ very remarkably from these.

INTRODUCTION OF TWO OR MORE INDEPENDENT VARIABLES.

8. It is convenient, in Simple Differential Equations, to contemplate one quantity z as expressed algebraically in terms of another quantity x (whether it be actually so expressed, or not): and to consider its differential-coefficients

$$\frac{dz}{dx}, \quad \frac{d}{dx}\left(\frac{dz}{dx}\right) \text{ or } \frac{d^2z}{dx^2}, \quad \&c.,$$

as being formed by taking the limiting values of fractions, in each of which the denominator is an increment in the value of x, and the numerator is the corresponding increment of z, or of $\dfrac{dz}{dx}$, &c. And this is expressed by saying that x is the "independent variable." Geometrically it is illustrated by supposing that we consider an ordinate z of a plane curve, as also the inclination-tangent of the curve's-tangent, the change of that inclination-tangent for a small change in the value of x, &c., to be expressed in terms of the abscissa x.

9. There is no difficulty in conceiving z to depend on two quantities x and y, combined in any way and with any constants under any functional formula; and in considering that we may at pleasure change the value of x without changing that of y, or may change the value of y without changing that of x, or may change both simultaneously. If we do not vary y, y is *pro tempore* a constant : and by varying x alone, we may form $\dfrac{dz}{dx}$, $\dfrac{d^2z}{dx^2}$, &c., just as in the

functions which we have illustrated by reference to a plane curve. If we do not vary x, then x is *pro tempore* a constant, and by varying y alone, we may form $\dfrac{dz}{dy}$, $\dfrac{d^2z}{dy^2}$, &c. But if we vary both x and y, then we have the two series of differential-coefficients which we have just set down, and also $\dfrac{d^2z}{dx \cdot dy}$ or $\dfrac{d^2z}{dy \cdot dx}$ (which, as is known in the expansions obtained by the Differential Calculus, have the same value), with other coefficients of analogous form, which do not appear in the succession of coefficients, such as those of Article 8. Here we consider x and y as "two independent variables," which are strictly independent of each other : and z as a function of both.

10. Algebraical Geometry of three dimensions assists greatly in illustrating these algebraical conceptions. If x, y, z be three rectangular co-ordinates, then the expression of z by means of x and y determines the numerical value of the height of an ordinate z that must be erected over the point on the plane xy, which is defined by any numerical values of x and y, in order that the elevation of the summit of that ordinate z may represent the value of our algebraical function. If we do this for an infinite number of values of x and y, we determine an infinite number of ordinate-summits, all which lie in one curved-surface. If, supposing this curved-surface formed, we then contemplate the values of z with x invariable and y variable, we shall include all these values which are in a plane parallel

to the plane yz, and at the given distance x from the origin of co-ordinates. This is the same as forming a section of the curved-surface by a plane parallel to the plane yz, and considering the curved-intersection as an ordinary plane-curve. Thus we can obtain $\dfrac{dz}{dy}$, $\dfrac{d^2z}{dy^2}$, &c. as in Article 8: but it must be remembered that, in general, x is lurking in their expressions as a constant; and therefore, in the complete differentiation (with respect to x) of any formula in which they may occur, each must be considered as a function both of x and of y. Similarly, the values of z with y invariable and x variable will be formed by a section of the curved-surface, made by a plane parallel to xz: the differential-coefficients $\dfrac{dz}{dx}$, $\dfrac{d^2z}{dx^2}$, &c. can be formed; and a similar caution with regard to their dependence both on x and on y must be borne in mind.

11. The coefficients $\dfrac{dz}{dx}$, $\dfrac{d^2z}{dx^2}$, &c. are, as in Article 8, to be considered as defining the inclination-tangent of the curve's-tangent, the change of that inclination-tangent for a small change in the value of x, &c., &c., in the curve formed by the intersection of the plane parallel to xz with the curved-surface. In like manner, the coefficients $\dfrac{dz}{dy}$, $\dfrac{d^2z}{dy^2}$, &c. define similar elements in the curve formed by the intersection of the plane parallel to yz with the curved-surface. But the coefficient $\dfrac{d^2z}{dx\,.\,dy}$ requires further

explanation. Its real expression is $\frac{d}{dx}\left(\frac{dz}{dy}\right)$. Now $\frac{dz}{dy}$ defines the inclination-tangent of the curve's-tangent in the sectional plane parallel to yz: and therefore its differential-coefficient with respect to x defines the rate at which that inclination-tangent, in the plane parallel to yz, is changed by shifting the sectional-plane in the direction of x. Analogous explanations apply to analogous succeeding terms.

12. Algebraically, there is no difficulty in conceiving z as a function of any number of independent variables, as u, v, w, x, y, and in treating the various differential coefficients, which may rise to any degree of complexity. But we cannot extend any further the elucidation derived from Solid Geometry.

13. Although, in strictness, no difference is really made by any physical peculiarity in the nature of the quantities represented by the independent variables, provided that their magnitudes can be defined by numbers and can therefore be treated by algebraical process; yet it may be well to mention that, in some of the most important applications of Partial Differentials, one of the independent variables is the expression for *time*. Thus, suppose that we are considering the nature of the disturbance which each particle of air is undergoing in a musical pipe: we want to know the entire movements of the particle whose original ordinate was X; and this implies that, in the general formula for the disturbance, x (the general symbol of

X) is to have the special value for that particle, and is therefore to be made constant for that particle, but that no limit is to be put on the variations of t. We also want to know the state of disturbance of all the particles at a certain time T, and this implies that t is then to be made constant, but that x is to admit of all possible variation. And these can only be comprehended in a general formula which admits of variations both of x and of t. Similarly for the motion of the particles of waves of water, &c.; &c.

14. In Simple Differential Equations, the data of the problem, whether mechanical or geometrical, usually, lead to an equation between x, z, $\dfrac{dz}{dx}$, $\dfrac{d^2z}{dx^2}$, &c., from which we desire to obtain a general expression for z in terms of x. Similarly, in Partial Differential Equations the data of the problem usually lead to an equation between x, y, z, $\dfrac{dz}{dx}$, $\dfrac{dz}{dy}$, $\dfrac{d^2z}{dx^2}$, $\dfrac{d^2z}{dx \cdot dy}$, $\dfrac{d^2z}{dy^2}$, &c. from which we desire to obtain a general expression for z in terms of x and y. It is the object of the present treatise to shew how this may be done, and how the meaning of the solutions may be explained, in some of the simpler cases: and we now proceed with the Solution of Partial Differential Equations of the First Order.

TREATMENT OF THE SIMPLEST PARTIAL DIFFERENTIAL EQUATION OF THE FIRST ORDER.

15. The simplest Partial Differential Equation of the first order is

$$\frac{dz}{dx} = a\frac{dz}{dy}, \qquad \text{or } \frac{dz}{dx} - a\frac{dz}{dy} = 0.$$

[Here, and in all subsequent operations, we shall put u for $ax + y$.]

Evidently this equation is satisfied by making $z = u$. For $\dfrac{du}{dx} = a$, $\dfrac{du}{dy} = 1$, and therefore $\dfrac{du}{dx} - a\dfrac{du}{dy} = 0$. But it is also satisfied by making $z = \phi(u)$, where ϕ expresses a function whose form is totally unlimited. For then

$$\frac{dz}{dx} = \phi'(u) \cdot \frac{du}{dx} = \phi'(u) \times a;$$

$$\frac{dz}{dy} = \phi'(u) \cdot \frac{du}{dy} = \phi'(u) \times 1;$$

and therefore

$$\frac{dz}{dx} - a\frac{dz}{dy} = \phi'(u) \cdot \{a - a\} = 0.$$

16. We have thus found a solution of considerable generality in form; but there is no evidence that the generality is complete. In order to obtain complete and certain generality, we shall use a process of Change of Independent Variable, guiding ourselves in the selection of a new Independent Variable by the indications derived from the last imperfect process.

17.   Instead of considering z as a function of x and y, let us consider z as a function of x and u. [Such a supposition is certainly competent to represent z, because, if we had z expressed by x and y, we have merely to substitute for y its value $u - ax$, and z then becomes expressed by x and u.] Having z then a function of x and u, where u is itself a function of x and y, we proceed to express the original equation in terms of the new differential-coefficients. We shall put $\dfrac{d(z)}{dx}$ for the entire differential-coefficient in regard to every way in which x could appear when x and y were used, and $\dfrac{dz}{dx}$ for the differential-coefficient when x and u are used: the original equation is therefore to be written

$$\frac{d(z)}{dx} - a\,\frac{dz}{dy} = 0.$$

18. z is a function of x and u, where u depends on x and y.

Therefore

$$\frac{d(z)}{dx} = \frac{dz}{dx} + \frac{dz}{du}\cdot\frac{du}{dx} = \frac{dz}{dx} + \frac{dz}{du}\times a\,;$$

and

$$\frac{dz}{dy} = \frac{dz}{du}\cdot\frac{du}{dy} = \frac{dz}{du}\times 1.$$

Substituting these in the equation which is to be solved,

$$0 = \frac{d(z)}{dx} - a\,\frac{dz}{dy} = \frac{dz}{dx}.$$

That is to say, *when z is expressed in terms of x and u,*

$$\frac{dz}{dx} = 0.$$

The integration of this simple quantity involves the most important considerations of the whole theory.

19.   By the ordinary rules of integration, $z = C$, where C is something which does not contain x.   But what may it contain? It may contain every thing whatever except x. It may contain any constants whatever. It may contain u: for the differentiation with respect to x will not touch u, which is another Independent Variable and is a constant with respect to x.   It may contain any function of u.   It may contain these included in the form

"any function of constants and u."

But, in ordinary algebraical language, this would be sufficiently described as " any function of u," provided that we bear in mind that u may be combined with any constants, and may even actually disappear, so as to leave constants only. This being understood, the solution of the equation is

$$z = \phi(u),$$
$$\text{or } z = \phi(ax + y),$$

where ϕ expresses a function of any form whatever which considerations not yet presented to us may induce us to adopt.

The steps of this process leave no opening for further generality in the solution : which is therefore complete.

20. Instead of assuming z to be expressed by x and u, with elimination of y, we might have assumed z to be expressed by y and u, with elimination of x. Then the process is

$$\frac{d(z)}{dy} = \frac{dz}{dy} + \frac{dz}{du} \cdot \frac{du}{dy} = \frac{dz}{dy} + \frac{dz}{du} \times 1,$$

$$\frac{dz}{dx} = \frac{dz}{du} \cdot \frac{du}{dx} = \frac{dz}{du} \times a,$$

and

$$0 = \frac{dz}{dx} - a\frac{d(z)}{dy} = -a\frac{dz}{dy};$$

from which the same conclusion follows, namely

$$z = \phi(u) = \phi(ax + y).$$

21. We may even change the Independent Variables so as to eliminate both x and y; and, as this process will be important hereafter, we shall shew its application here. Let $u = ax + y$, $v = ex + fy$, where e is not equal to af; and let z be supposed to be expressed in terms of u and v.

Then

$$\frac{dz}{dx} = \frac{dz}{du} \cdot \frac{du}{dx} + \frac{dz}{dv} \cdot \frac{dv}{dx} = \frac{dz}{du} \times a + \frac{dz}{dv} \times e;$$

$$\frac{dz}{dy} = \frac{dz}{du} \cdot \frac{du}{dy} + \frac{dz}{dv} \cdot \frac{dv}{dy} = \frac{dz}{du} \times 1 + \frac{dz}{dv} \times f;$$

and the equation

$$\frac{dz}{dx} - a\frac{dz}{dy} = 0$$

becomes

$$(e - af)\frac{dz}{dv} = 0, \quad \text{or } \frac{dz}{d\tau} = 0 ;$$

whence, in the same manner as before,

$$z = \phi(u) = \phi(ax + y).$$

GEOMETRICAL INTERPRETATION OF THE SOLUTION.

22. In order to shew the geometrical meaning of this, by reference to such a curved-surface as has been considered in Articles 10 and 11, we may observe that if δx and δy are exceedingly small increments of x and y, then the increment of $z = \frac{dz}{dx}\delta x + \frac{dz}{dy}\delta y$; which, since $\frac{dz}{dx} = a\frac{dz}{dy}$, becomes $\frac{dz}{dy}(a\delta x + \delta y)$; and, if we always make $\delta y = -a\delta x$, the increment of z will be $= 0$; that is, if we always pass from one point on the plane xy to another point on that plane by a short line making with the axis of x the angle whose trigonometrical-tangent is a (which process continually repeated will produce a finite straight line in the same direction), the value of z will be invariable. Therefore, the curve-surface will consist of a series of parallel lines, in each of which the values of z are the same so long as $ax + y$ is the same, but which is subject to no other condition. It will therefore be such as is represented in figure 1; a cylindrical surface (in the widest sense of the word),

whose axis is parallel to xy and makes with x the angle whose trigonometrical-tangent is a, but whose transversal section, or section by either of the planes xz, yz, is absolutely undefined by the equation. Those sections may be adapted to specific physical data, and are therefore of the nature of the quantities which we call *undetermined*. But, as the only condition at present established is that the lines (of which the surface consists) shall be parallel, the sections need not to consist of curves defined each by a single equation in its whole extent. A section may consist of a bit of a circle with a bit of a cissoid and then a bit of a logarithmic spiral; and these may be joined at any angles; or the section may be utterly undefinable by algebra: and after it has gone on to some extent, there may be an absolute interruption and then it may begin again, &c.

CHARACTERISTICS OF THE SOLUTIONS OF PARTIAL DIFFERENTIAL EQUATIONS.

23.   Thus it appears that these conditions hold in the solution;

It is not certain that one symbolic expression will represent the solution, or that one curve defined by one equation will represent the section of the curve-surface.

It is not certain that the section is continuous, either as to actual connexion of parts, or as to gradual change of direction, or in any other circumstance.

There may be isolated parts of the curve, of totally distinct character.

An undetermined quantity must be introduced : but this undetermined quantity will not usually be a simple constant, but will be a function of x and y, and (in the most general case) a discontinuous function, such as corresponds to the discontinuity of curve mentioned in Article 22.

On comparing these conditions with those in Article 5, the reader will see the characteristic differences between the solutions of Simple and of Partial Differential Equations.

INTERPRETATION OF THE SOLUTION WHEN ONE INDEPENDENT VARIABLE IS TIME.

24. There is another instance of the solution in Article 19, &c. or (more frequently) of a solution of the same form in the treatment of Partial Differential Equations of the Second Order, which merits explanation. Let one of the Independent Variables be time : put t for y, and suppose the function of $t + ax$ to be $\psi \{b(t + ax)\}$ or $\psi(bt + cx)$, c being $= ba$. Then $z = \psi(bt + cx)$. Let any one value of $bt + cx$ be B: then if t be increased by cC (where C is really arbitrary), and if x be increased by $-bC$, the value of $bt + cx$ is still $= B$, and therefore z remains the same. That is, at a time later by cC, we shall have the same value of z, provided that we take an abscissa smaller by bC. This is just the same as if the ordinate z was slid backwards upon the abscissa x with a velocity

represented by $\dfrac{bC}{cC}$, or $\dfrac{b}{c}$. The same applies to every other

ordinate z. And thus it appears that the whole curve defined by the summits of z may be conceived as changing its shape by sliding backwards with a definite velocity $\dfrac{b}{c}$.

This is the characteristic of a *wave,* in which (as in waves of water, to take the most familiar instance) the form travels while the particles do not travel with the form. Whenever therefore we meet with such a term as $\phi(ax + y)$ we may at once take for granted that one of its applications may be to the motion of a wave.

If the value of z had been $\psi(bt - cx)$, we should have found in like manner that the wave is travelling forwards.

These remarks do not in any degree interfere with those of Article 23.

OTHER PARTIAL DIFFERENTIAL EQUATIONS OF THE FIRST ORDER.

25. We proceed with the equation $\dfrac{dz}{dx} - a\dfrac{dz}{dy} = \alpha(x, y)$, where the form of the function α is given. We shall solve it by the method of Change of Independent Variables. Let $u = ax + y$, $v = ex + fy$, where e is not equal to af, (which, by giving different values to e and f, includes the three changes in Articles 19, 20, 21). The value of x in terms of u and v is $\dfrac{fu - v}{af - e}$, that of y is $\dfrac{-eu + av}{af - e}$. Treat-

ing the equation as in Article 21, we find

$$(e - af) \frac{dz}{dv} = a\,(x, y) = a\left(\frac{fu - v}{af - e}, \; \frac{-eu + av}{af - e}\right);$$

whence, integrating on the same principles as before,

$$z = \phi\,(u) + \frac{1}{e - af}\int_v a\left(\frac{fu - v}{af - e}, \; \frac{-eu + av}{af - e}\right);$$

where, in the integration with respect to v, u is to be considered constant; and, after the integration, $ax + y$ and $ex + fy$ are to be substituted for u and v.

26.   On trying this process upon any ordinary function (as a function in integral powers of x and y, or a circular or exponential function) of which the integrations are easy, it will be found that e and f disappear from the result.   It may be well to shew this in a simple instance.

Let one term of $a\,(x, y)$ be $x^p . y^q$.

The corresponding term of the integral is

$$\frac{-1}{(af - e)^{p+q+1}}\int_v \{(fu - v)^p . (-eu + av)^q\}.$$

Integrate by parts, beginning with the first factor; it gives

$$\frac{+1}{(p + 1) . (af - e)^{p+q+1}}(fu - v)^{p+1} . (-eu + av)^q$$

$$-\frac{aq}{(p + 1) . (af - e)^{p+q+1}}\int_v (fu - v)^{p+1} . (-eu + av)^{q-1}$$

$$= \frac{1}{p+1} x^{p+1} . y^q - \frac{aq}{(p+1).(af-e)^{p+q+1}} \int_v (fu-v)^{p+1} . (eu+av)^{q-1};$$

and, by repeating the process, we shall obtain the result in $q+1$ terms, in powers of x and y, and without e and f.

27. If we had begun the integration-by-parts with integration of the second factor, we should have obtained a different series of terms of powers of x and y; yet the difference would have been such as to produce no difference in the final result, as applicable to any physical investigation in which the undetermined function is to be adapted to given physical circumstances. A simple instance will shew this.

Let $\alpha(x,y) = x . y^2$. Then we obtain the two following series for the integral:

First,

$$z = \phi(ax+y) + \frac{1}{12a^2} \{6a^2 x^2 y^2 + 4a^3 x^3 y + a^4 x^4\}.$$

Second,

$$z = \psi(ax+y) + \frac{1}{12a^2} \{ - 4axy^3 - y^4\}.$$

The second value, it is easily seen, may be put under the form

$$\psi(ax+y) + \frac{1}{12a^2} \{6a^2 x^2 y^2 + 4a^3 x^3 y + a^4 x^4\}$$

$$- \frac{1}{12a^2} \{y^4 + 4axy^3 + 6a^2 x^2 y^2 + 4a^3 x^3 y + a^4 x^4\}$$

$$= \psi \, (ax + y) - \frac{1}{12a^2} (ax + y)^4$$

$$+ \frac{1}{12a^2} \{6a^2 x^2 y^2 + 4a^3 x^3 y + a^4 x^4\}.$$

Now $- \dfrac{1}{12a^2} (ax + y)^4$ is a function of $(ax + y)$; and, when we proceed to determine the form of the function $\psi \, (ax + y)$, which must be adopted, in order, with the other terms of the expression, to satisfy any condition prescribed by physical considerations, we must at the same time take into account $- \dfrac{1}{12a^2} (ax + y)^4$ as a function of $(ax + y)$.   We may therefore at once unite it with $\psi \, (ax + y)$.   Call their sum $\chi \, (ax + y)$.   Then the second solution is

$$z = \chi \, (ax + y) + \frac{1}{12a^2} (6a^2 x^2 y^2 + 4a^3 x^3 y + a^4 x^4);$$

precisely the same as the first, except that the symbol χ stands in the place of ϕ.   But in both cases the form of the function ϕ or χ will be determined by the consideration of satisfying the same physical condition.   And therefore, whether we write ϕ or χ, we shall afterwards arrive at the same expressions; and therefore the two solutions, first and second, are in use identical.

28.   In many cases, when the form of solution has been obtained by the process of Article 25, the details will be obtained most readily by assuming the form of solution with indeterminate coefficients.

29.　It is not intended here to go into any discussion of the more complicated forms of Partial Differential Equations of the first order. The following however may be mentioned as flowing immediately from the solutions which we have found.

$$\text{If } \frac{dz}{dx} - a\frac{dz}{dy} = \beta(z) \times \alpha(x, y), \text{ let } \frac{1}{\beta(z)} = \gamma'(z),$$

and the equation is immediately reduced to the form already treated.

$$\text{If the first side is } \epsilon(x) \times \frac{dz}{dx} - a \times \zeta(y) \times \frac{dz}{dy},$$

$$\text{let } \frac{1}{\epsilon(x)} = \eta'(x) \text{ and } \frac{1}{\zeta(y)} = \theta'(y),$$

and the equation is reduced to the same form.

$$\text{If } \frac{dz}{dx} - a\frac{dz}{dy} = \kappa'(x), \text{ let } z_1 = z - \kappa(x); \text{ then}$$

$$\frac{dz_1}{dx} = \frac{dz}{dx} - \kappa'(x), \quad \frac{dz_1}{dy} = \frac{dz}{dy},$$

and the equation becomes

$$\frac{dz_1}{dx} - a\frac{dz_1}{dy} = 0.$$

In reference to physical investigations, the theory of Partial Differential Equations of the first order is principally valuable as introductory to that of the second order. In this view, it is hoped that the instances here given are sufficient.

TREATMENT OF THE SIMPLEST PARTIAL DIFFERENTIAL EQUATION OF THE SECOND ORDER.

30. The simplest Partial Differential Equation of the second order is

$$\frac{d^2 z}{dx \cdot dy} = 0.$$

Integrating with respect to x, and remarking that, by virtue of the reasoning in Article 19, there must be added to the integral an undetermined function of y,

$$\frac{dz}{dy} = \phi'(y).$$

Integrating this with respect to y, and remarking that, for the same reasons, an undetermined function of x must be added,

$$z = \phi(y) + \psi(x).$$

GEOMETRICAL INTERPRETATION OF THE SOLUTION.

31. This equation and its solution admit of easy geometrical illustration. Referring to Article 11, it will be seen that $\frac{dz}{dy}$ is the trigonometrical-tangent of the angle between y and the curve-tangent, in the curve formed by the intersection of a curved-surface with a plane parallel to zy. And the equation $\frac{d^2 z}{dx \cdot dy} = 0$, or $\frac{d}{dx}\left(\frac{dz}{dy}\right) = 0$, denotes that, when x is changed, $\frac{dz}{dy}$ undergoes no change; or that

the inclination in the plane zy will be the same for a point more or less advanced in the direction of x as for the point under consideration. The curve-tangent may be absolutely higher or lower in the direction of z, but it will preserve the same inclination to y. As this applies to every point of the intersection-curve, it follows that the intersection-curve more or less advanced in the direction of x will have the same form as that at the point under consideration; or that all sections by planes parallel to zy give the same curve, though perhaps at different elevations. And from this it follows (considering that, when two similar curves are separated ·in the direction of x, the slope from every point of one to the corresponding point of the other, in the direction of x, must be the same) that all sections by planes parallel to zx give the same curve, but not necessarily the same as those given by planes parallel to zy. Then the elevation of any point z may be considered as composed of these two parts; first, the elevation of the corresponding point of that zy curve whose plane passes through the origin, which elevation (since the form of the curve is the same for all values of x) may be called $\phi(y)$; secondly, the elevation of the point z above the point last considered, which elevation (since the points are connected by a curve whose form is independent of y) may be called $\psi(x)$. The whole elevation of the point z will therefore be

$$\phi(y) + \psi(x).$$

32. These functions may be discontinuous, for the reasons stated in Article 22.

33. In figure 2 is a representation of one of the solids in which $\phi(y)$ and $\psi(x)$ are both continuous functions. It is scarcely necessary to remark that the forms of such solids may be infinitely varied; thus (taking the vertex as origin of coordinates), if $z = \dfrac{x^2}{a} + \dfrac{y^2}{b}$, or both sections be parabolas with different parameters, the curve-surface is a paraboloid with elliptic base; if $z = \dfrac{x^2 + y^2}{a} = \dfrac{r^2}{a}$, the curve-surface is the paraboloid of revolution (from which, figure 2 was drawn); if $z = \dfrac{x^2}{a} - \dfrac{y^2}{b}$, the curve-surface is like a limited portion of the interior of an annulus, or like a mountain-pass, &c. &c. &c.

In figure 3 is a representation of a curve-surface in which one function is continuous (the sections being similar parabolas), the other is discontinuous (each section being two sides of a triangle, the triangle being the same throughout).

In figure 4 is a representation of a surface in which both functions are discontinuous (each section being two sides of a triangle, but the triangles in the plane xz being different from those in the plane yz). It forms, in fact, a pyramid with trapezoidal base; two vertices of the trapezium having the same value of x, and two having the same value of y, and the vertex of the pyramid being above the intersection of the diameters of the trapezium.

34. The solution of the equation $\dfrac{d^2z}{dx \cdot dy} = \alpha\,(x,\,y)$ obviously is,

$$z = \phi\,(y) + \psi\,(x) + \int_y \cdot \int_x \cdot \alpha\,(x, y).$$

TREATMENT OF ANOTHER PARTIAL DIFFERENTIAL EQUA-
TION OF THE SECOND ORDER.   FIRST, BY CHANGE OF
INDEPENDENT VARIABLES.

35. To solve the equation $\dfrac{d^2z}{dx^2} - a^2\dfrac{d^2z}{ay^2} = \alpha\,(x,\,y)$.
[This equation is the most important of all, especially in
reference to those physical theories in which wave-
transmission, of sound, or of light, or of water, &c., is
explained by mechanical theory.]

The best method of solving this equation is by the
Change of Independent Variables.

Let $\qquad\qquad u = ax + y, \; v = ax - y,$

$$\left(\text{which give } x = \frac{u+v}{2a},\, y = \frac{u-v}{2}\right).$$

Consider z as a function of x and y because it is a
function of u and v.

Then

$$\frac{dz}{dx} = \frac{dz}{du}\times\frac{du}{dx} + \frac{dz}{dv}\times\frac{dv}{dx} = \frac{dz}{du}\times a + \frac{dz}{dv}\times a;$$

$$\frac{d^2z}{dx^2} = \frac{d}{dx}\left(\frac{dz}{dx}\right) = \frac{d}{du}\left(\frac{dz}{dx}\right)\times\frac{du}{dx} + \frac{d}{dv}\left(\frac{dz}{dx}\right)\times\frac{dv}{dx}$$

$$= \frac{d}{du}\left(\frac{dz}{du}\times a + \frac{dz}{dv}\times a\right)\times a + \frac{d}{dv}\left(\frac{dz}{du}\times a + \frac{dz}{dv}\times a\right)\times a$$

$$= a^2\frac{d^2z}{du^2} + 2a^2\frac{d^2z}{du \cdot dv} + a^2\frac{d^2z}{dv^2}:$$

$$\frac{dz}{dy} = \frac{dz}{du}\times\frac{du}{dy} + \frac{dz}{dv}\times\frac{dv}{dy} = \frac{dz}{du}\times 1 + \frac{dz}{dv}\times -1;$$

$$\frac{d^2z}{dy^2} = \frac{d}{dy}\left(\frac{dz}{dy}\right) = \frac{d}{du}\left(\frac{dz}{dy}\right)\times\frac{du}{dy} + \frac{d}{dv}\left(\frac{dz}{dy}\right)\times\frac{dv}{dy}$$

$$= \frac{d}{du}\left(\frac{dz}{du}\times 1 + \frac{dz}{dv}\times -1\right)\times 1 + \frac{d}{dv}\left(\frac{dz}{du}\times 1 + \frac{dz}{dv}\times -1\right)\times -1$$

$$= \frac{d^2z}{du^2} - 2\frac{d^2z}{du \cdot dv} + \frac{d^2z}{dv^2}.$$

Hence
$$\frac{d^2z}{dx^2} - a^2\frac{d^2z}{dy^2} = 4a^2\frac{d^2z}{du \cdot dv}.$$

And the original equation, divided by $4a^2$, becomes

$$\frac{d^2z}{du \cdot dv} = \frac{1}{4a^2}\times \alpha\left(\frac{u+v}{2a}, \frac{u-v}{2}\right).$$

Whence, by Article 34,

$$z = \phi(v) + \psi(u) + \frac{1}{4a^2}\int_v \cdot \int_u \cdot \alpha\left(\frac{u+v}{2a}, \frac{u-v}{2}\right);$$

or $z = \phi(ax-y) + \psi(ax+y) + \dfrac{1}{4a^2}\displaystyle\int_v \cdot \int_u \cdot \alpha\left(\frac{u+v}{2a}, \frac{u-v}{2}\right);$

where, after the integration, for u and v are to be put $ax + y$ and $ax - y$.

35*. If the right-hand term of the given equation were a simple function of x, multiplied only by constants and the first power of y, as if

$$\frac{d^2 z}{dx^2} - a^2 \frac{d^2 z}{dy^2} = (b + cy) \times \beta''(x),$$

let
$$z_1 = z - (b + cy) \times \beta(x):$$

then
$$\frac{d^2 z_1}{dx^2} = \frac{d^2 z}{dx^2} - (b + cy) \times \beta'(x), \frac{d^2 z_1}{dy^2} = \frac{d^2 z}{dy^2};$$

and the equation becomes

$$\frac{d^2 z_1}{dx^2} - a^2 \frac{d^2 z_1}{dy^2} = 0;$$

of which the solution (by the formula above, when $\alpha = 0$) is
$$z_1 = \phi(ax - y) + \psi(ax + y);$$

or
$$z = \phi(ax - y) + \psi(ax + y) + (b + cy) \times \beta(x).$$

35**. When $\alpha = 0$, the solution $z = \phi(u) + \psi(v)$ may be represented geometrically in the same manner as $z = \phi(x) + \psi(y)$ in Article 33, with this difference only, that u and v are ordinates on the plane xy, which are not at right angles, except in the case when $a = 1$.

36. When one of the independent variables is time, it will be seen by the same reasoning as in Article 24 that the two undetermined functions represent two waves travelling in opposite directions.

SECOND TREATMENT OF THE SAME EQUATION, BY SEPARA-
TION OF THE SYMBOLS OF OPERATION FROM THOSE
OF QUANTITY.

37. A second method of solving the equation

$$\frac{d^2z}{dx^2} - a^2\frac{d^2z}{dy^2} = \alpha(x, y)$$

is founded upon the "separation of the symbols of operation from those of quantity." This theory is, in fact,
merely a convenient form for exhibiting the indubitable
results of legitimate algebra; but it sometimes serves to
suggest new methods of treating equations, which, when
verified, are useful.

38. The equation

$$\frac{dz}{dx} + a\frac{dz}{dy} = (X, Y)$$

may be written, almost without departure from ordinary
notation,

$$\left(\frac{d}{dx} + a\frac{d}{dy}\right) z = (X, Y);$$

the connexion of the left-hand bracket with z which follows
it being, however, not by multiplication but by differentiation. And, if

$$\frac{d(X, Y)}{dx} - a\frac{d(X, Y)}{dy} = \alpha(x, y),$$

we may, on the same principle, write it

$$\left(\frac{d}{dx} - a\frac{d}{dy}\right)(X,\ Y) \ = \ \alpha\,(x, y)\,;$$

and therefore

$$\left(\frac{d}{dx} - a\frac{d}{dy}\right)\left(\frac{d}{dx} + a\frac{d}{dy}\right) z \ = \ \alpha\,(x, y)\,;$$

still on the understanding that the connexions on the left hand are not by multiplication but by differentiation.

39. Now, if we treated all the left-hand symbols as signs not of operation but of quantity, their product would be

$$\left(\frac{d^2}{dx^2} - a^2\frac{d^2}{dy^2}\right) z\,;$$

or, pursuing the fanciful idea still further,

$$\frac{d^2 z}{dx^2} - a^2\frac{d^2 z}{dy^2}\,;$$

and this suggests the idea that, if we follow up the true differential operations instead of the fanciful algebraical multiplications, we shall arrive at that result in its true differential meaning: And so, in fact, it proves. For, by actual differentiation,

$$\frac{d}{dx}\left(\frac{dz}{dx} + a\frac{dz}{dy}\right) \ = \ \frac{d^2 z}{dx^2} + a\frac{d^2 z}{dx\,.\,dy}\,;$$

$$-\,a \times \frac{d}{dy}\left(\frac{dz}{dx} + a\frac{dz}{dy}\right) \ = \ -\,a\frac{d^2 z}{dx\,.\,dy} - a^2\frac{d^2 z}{dy^2}\,;$$

and, adding the two lines,

$$\left(\frac{d}{dx} - a\,\frac{d}{dy}\right)\left(\frac{dz}{dx} + a\,\frac{dz}{dy}\right) = \frac{d^2z}{dx^2} - a^2\,\frac{d^2z}{dy^2}.$$

Here the analogy with the algebraical operation has led to a real gain of convenience, by shewing that we can here break up the operation for a Partial Differential Equation of the second order into two operations for the first order.

40. Thus, to solve the equation

$$\frac{d^2z}{dx^2} - a^2\frac{d^2z}{dy^2} = \alpha\,(x, y),$$

we have first to solve the equation

$$\frac{d(X,\ Y)}{dx} - a\frac{d(X,\ Y)}{dy} = \alpha\,(x, y);$$

from which $(X,\ Y)$ will be found; and then to solve the equation

$$\frac{dz}{dx} + a\frac{dz}{dy} = (X,\ Y),$$

from which z will be found.

Both operations are effected by the process of Article 25; the most convenient assumption however being

$$u = ax + y, \quad v = ax - y.$$

We shall return hereafter to the "separation of symbols."

OTHER PARTIAL DIFFERENTIAL EQUATIONS OF THE SECOND ORDER.

41.   To solve the equation

$$\frac{d^2z}{dx^2} + a^2\frac{d^2z}{dy^2} = 0,$$

or

$$\frac{d^2z}{dx^2} - (a\sqrt{-1})^2 . \frac{d^2z}{dy^2} = 0.$$

It does not appear possible to solve this equation generally, except by the use of imaginary symbols.   If we take the second form of the equation (as written above), and apply the solution of Articles 35, &c.

$$z = \phi\,(y + a\sqrt{-1}\,.\,x) + \psi\,(y - a\sqrt{-1}\,.\,x).$$

If, as is usual, we suppose ϕ and ψ to represent real functions, it will be impossible to destroy the imaginary terms in this expression except by making ψ the same as ϕ, and thus giving up part of the generality of the solution. But the introduction of two undetermined functions may be thus obtained.   Let

$$\phi = \chi + \sqrt{-1}\,.\,\omega, \quad \psi = \chi - \sqrt{-1}\,.\,\omega,$$

where χ and ω are real functions.

Then

$$z = \chi\,(y + a\sqrt{-1}\,.\,x) + \chi\,(y - a\sqrt{-1}\,.\,x)$$
$$+ \sqrt{-1}\,.\,\omega\,(y + a\sqrt{-1}\,.\,x) - \sqrt{-1}\,.\,\omega\,(y - a\sqrt{-1}\,.\,x).$$

Expanding the functions by Taylor's Theorem, it will be seen that the imaginary terms are destroyed, and there are two undetermined functions.

It will be seen hereafter that, in some practical applications of this equation under limiting conditions, the solution may be obtained more easily by specific process than by using the general solution.

42. The following equation, which occurred to the author in the investigation of the movement of spherical waves of air (gravity being neglected), deserves attention for the nature of the substitutions made and the form of the result.

The equation given by the physical considerations is,

$$\frac{d^2z}{dt^2} = a^2 \cdot \frac{d}{dx}\left(\frac{2z}{x} + \frac{dz}{dx}\right).$$

The last term may be made simpler by assuming

$$z = \frac{d}{dx}\left(\frac{y}{x}\right),$$

or

$$y = x\int_x z.$$

Differentiating this twice with respect to x,

$$\frac{d^2y}{dx^2} = 2z + x\frac{dz}{dx};$$

and

$$\frac{1}{x} \cdot \frac{d^2y}{dx^2} = \frac{2z}{x} + \frac{dz}{dx};$$

whence the second side of the equation

$$= a^2 \cdot \frac{d}{dx}\left(\frac{1}{x} \cdot \frac{d^2y}{dx^2}\right).$$

For the first side, or $\dfrac{d^2z}{dt^2}$, we have

$$\frac{d^2z}{dt^2} = \frac{d^2}{dt^2} \cdot \frac{d}{dx} \cdot \left(\frac{y}{x}\right) = \frac{d}{dx} \cdot \frac{d^2}{dt^2}\left(\frac{y}{x}\right);$$

which, since $\dfrac{y}{x}$ can be affected by $\dfrac{d^2}{dt^2}$ only because y is a function of t, becomes

$$\frac{d}{dx}\left(\frac{1}{x} \cdot \frac{d^2y}{dt^2}\right);$$

and the original equation is changed to

$$\frac{d}{dx}\left(\frac{1}{x} \cdot \frac{d^2y}{dt^2}\right) - a^2 \cdot \frac{d}{dx}\left(\frac{1}{x} \cdot \frac{d^2y}{dx^2}\right) = 0.$$

Integrating with respect to x,

$$\frac{1}{x} \cdot \frac{d^2y}{dt^2} - \frac{a^2}{x} \cdot \frac{d^2y}{dx^2} = \chi''(t),$$

or

$$\frac{d^2y}{dt^2} - a^2 \frac{d^2y}{dx^2} = x \cdot \chi''(t).$$

Solving this by the method of Article 35[*],

$$y = x \cdot \chi(t) + \phi(at+x) + \psi(at-x);$$

whence

$$z = \frac{d}{dx}\left(\frac{y}{x}\right) = -\frac{1}{x^2}\phi(at+x) + \frac{1}{x}\phi'(at+x) - \frac{1}{x^2}\psi(at-x)$$

$$-\frac{1}{x}\psi'(at-x).$$

42*. In the Author's Treatise on Sound, Article 43 and several following articles, will be found a discussion of equations of the form

$$\frac{1}{a^2}\cdot\frac{d^2W}{dt^2} = \frac{d^2W}{dr^2} + \frac{m}{r}\cdot\frac{dW}{dr},$$

where m has different integral values.

43. We believe that scarcely any other equations than these, occurring in physical investigations, have been solved in a finite form. Several equations have been solved in the unsatisfactory form of infinite series, of which the convergence is not always assured; but it is not the object of the present Treatise to enter on them.

44. The following equations which have presented themselves in the author's investigations, (probably among many others occurring in physical inquiries), have not been solved.

In investigating the vertical motion of a horizontal wave of air, on the supposition that the elasticity is proportional to the density, and that gravity is constant, we arrive at an equation of this form:

$$\frac{d^2X}{dx^2} - a\frac{dX}{dx} - b^2\frac{d^2X}{at^2} = 0;$$

D. E.   D

which we have not succeeded in integrating generally in a finite form.

In investigating the radial motion of a spherical wave of air whose center is the center of the earth, supposing the elasticity to be as the nth power of the density (where n must be greater than a certain quantity which is > 1, in order to make the whole mass of atmosphere finite), the resulting equation takes this form:

$$\left\{ A - \frac{(n-1)\,a^2}{r} \right\} \frac{d}{dr}\left(\frac{dR}{dr} + 2\,\frac{R}{r}\right) + \frac{na^2}{r^i}\left(\frac{dR}{dr} + 2\,\frac{R}{r}\right)$$

$$+ b^2 \frac{d^2 R}{dt^2} - \frac{4a^2 R}{r^3} = 0.$$

This equation may be much simplified, but in any form we have not rendered it integrable.

FURTHER CONSIDERATION OF THE SEPARATION OF THE SYMBOLS OF OPERATION FROM THOSE OF QUANTITY.

45. In Article 39 attention was called to the method of solving the equation then under consideration by the "Separation of the symbols of operation from those of quantity." This principle may be applied to an extensive system of equations, which are however, at present, matters rather of curiosity than of physical value. It may be sufficient here to indicate one class.

If the equation

$$\frac{d^n z}{dx^n} + A\frac{d^n z}{dx^{n-1}\, dy} + B\frac{d^n z}{dx^{n-2}\, dy^2} + \ldots\ldots + L\frac{d^n z}{dy^n} = \alpha\,(x,\, y)$$

can be expressed as

$$\left(\frac{d}{dx} - a\frac{d}{dy}\right) \times \left(\frac{d}{dx} - b\frac{d}{dy}\right) \times \&\text{c. to } n \text{ terms} \times z = \alpha\,(x,\, y),$$

then the process of Article 40 can be applied with so little difficulty that it appears unnecessary for us to delay further on it. In the successive changes of Independent Variable, it will be found convenient to take the factors in successive pairs; thus, for the effect of the first pair of factors, where

$$\left(\frac{d}{dx} - a\frac{d}{dy}\right)\left(\frac{d}{dx} - b\frac{d}{dy}\right)(X,\, Y) = \alpha\,(x,\, y),$$

assume $\qquad ax + y = u, \quad bx + y = v,$

and proceed as in Article 25.

46. There is one exceptional case, however, well brought to notice by this method of treatment, which merits further attention; namely, that in which two factors $a,\, b,$ are equal. To take the simplest case, suppose

$$\frac{d^2 z}{dx^2} - 2a\frac{d^2 z}{dx\,dy} + a^2\frac{d^2 z}{dy^2} = 0,$$

or
$$\left(\frac{d}{dx} - a\frac{d}{dy}\right)\left(\frac{d}{dx} - a\frac{d}{dy}\right) z = 0.$$

Here we may assume $ax + y = u$, $ex + fy = v$, e and f being any constants whatever whose proportion is not $a : 1$; the value 0 being admissible for either.

Then
$$\frac{d(X, Y)}{dx} = \frac{d(X, Y)}{du} \times a + \frac{d(X, Y)}{dv} \times e;$$

$$\frac{d(X, Y)}{dy} = \frac{d(X, Y)}{du} \times 1 + \frac{d(X, Y)}{dv} \times f;$$

and, putting (X, Y) for $\left(\frac{d}{dx} - a\frac{d}{dy}\right) z$,

the equation $\qquad \left(\frac{d}{dx} - a\frac{d}{dy}\right)(X, Y) = 0,$

becomes $\qquad (e - af)\dfrac{d(X, Y)}{dv} = 0;$

whence $\qquad (X, Y) = \phi(u).$

And, putting for (X, Y) its value,

$$\left(\frac{d}{dx} - a\frac{d}{dy}\right) z = \phi(u);$$

or, by the same substitution which was made in regard to the differential coefficients of (X, Y),

$$(e - af)\frac{dz}{dv} = \phi(u);$$

integrating this, and remarking that $\phi(u)$ possesses the properties of a constant as regards integration with respect to v,

$$(e - af)\, z = v \cdot \phi(u) + \psi(u);$$

or

$$z = \left(\frac{f}{e - af} y + \frac{e}{e - af} x \right) \cdot \phi(y + ax) + \psi(y + ax).$$

Observing that a constant factor may be supposed to be included in the form of an undetermined function, we may express z in either of the forms,

$$(gy + hx) \times \phi(y + ax) + \psi(y + ax);$$

$$y \times \phi_1(y + ax) + \psi_1(y + ax);$$

$$x \times \phi_2(y + ax) + \psi_2(y + ax);$$

all which, as applicable to the satisfaction of any assigned conditions, will be found to be identical, on employing the reasoning of Article 27.

47.   In pursuing this subject, the signs $\int$ and d may be considered as reciprocal, or $\int = d^{-1}$.   In some cases, equations may be varied by carrying symbols, such as

$$\frac{d}{dx} - a\frac{d}{dy},$$

which hold the position of multiplier on one side of the equation, to the position of divisor on the other side, or as multiplier in the form

$$\left(\frac{d}{dx} - a\,\frac{d}{dy}\right)^{-1}.$$

And in this shape they may be substituted in abstruse and general theorems. For instance, to take a case which (in this theory) is almost elementary, we know that

$$\left(\frac{d}{dx}\right)^{n}\left(u\,\epsilon^{ax}\right) = \epsilon^{ax}\left(\frac{d^n u}{dx^n} + \frac{n}{1}\,a\,\frac{d^{n-1}u}{dx^{n-1}} + \&\mathrm{c.}\right)$$

$$= \epsilon^{ax}\left(\frac{d}{dx} + a\right)^{n} u.$$

If $n = -1$, this becomes, reversing the sides of the equation,

$$\epsilon^{ax}\left(\frac{d}{dx} + a\right)^{-1} u = \int_{x} u\,\epsilon^{ax},$$

$$\text{or }\left(\frac{d}{dx} + a\right)^{-1} u = \epsilon^{-ax}\int_{x} u\,\epsilon^{ax}.$$

But the equation

$$\frac{dz}{dx} + e\,\frac{dz}{dy} = u,$$

$$\text{or }\left(\frac{d}{dx} + e\,\frac{d}{dy}\right) z = u,$$

may, in accordance with these principles, be put in the form

$$z = \left(\frac{d}{dx} + e\,\frac{d}{dy}\right)^{-1} u;$$

and the second side agrees with the first side above, provided that $e\dfrac{d}{dy}$ be put for a and treated as a constant.

Then we shall have

$$z = \epsilon^{-e\frac{d}{dy}x} \int_x u\, \epsilon^{e\frac{d}{dy}x} \; ;$$

a solution to which, in some cases, a real meaning may be given.

48. This principle, as a purely algebraical and symbolical process, possesses very great power, and leads to very remarkable results. But the reader cannot fail to observe that it carries with it no evidence whatever for the validity of results (such as is conveyed by the operations of quantitative algebra, or by the steps, properly pursued, of the differential calculus), for which it must rely on subsequent verifications. As aiding the application of Partial Differential Equations to physical investigations it possesses little value. The further examination of it would therefore be out of place in this Treatise. The student who desires to follow it up will find much information in Boole's *Treatise on Differential Equations*, Gregory's *Examples*, and similar works.

TREATMENT OF PARTIAL DIFFERENTIAL EQUATIONS WHEN THE SOLUTION IS LIMITED BY PREARRANGED CONDITIONS.

49. We have seen in Article 44 that there are some Partial Differential Equations of which the solutions cannot be obtained by known methods, so long as the utmost generality is required in the solutions. But in some cases, by attaching limiting conditions to the solutions, the same equations may be integrated with ease; as will be seen in the following instances.

50. In considering the tidal disturbance of water in an equatoreal canal round the earth, retarded by friction proportional to the velocity (see the *Encyclopædia Metropolitana*, Article *Tides and Waves*), we arrive at the following equation (x the original ordinate of a particle measured along the canal, X the horizontal disturbance of the particle):

$$\frac{d^2 X}{dt^2} = H \sin (it - mx) - f \frac{dX}{dt} + a^2 \frac{d^2 X}{dx^2};$$

where H, f, a^2, are constants depending on the moon's attraction, the coefficient of friction, and the depth of the sea. This equation cannot be solved generally. But, remarking that the only part of the solution which has any interest for us is that which follows the same law of periodicity as the lunar motions, we may assume

$$X = A \sin (it - mx) + B \cos (it - mx),$$

where A and B are constants to be determined. On substituting this, the values of A and B and the expression for X are found without difficulty.

51. Before adverting to a specific solution of the equation $\dfrac{d^2z}{dx^2} + a^2 \dfrac{d^2z}{dy^2} = 0$, we will make the following remark on the general solution. When an exponential form is adopted for the functions in the general solution, Article 41, the general form may be retained conveniently: but in other cases it is usually necessary to expand the functions. Performing this process according to the ordinary algebraical rules, the general solution becomes

$$\chi(y) - \chi''(y)\frac{a^2x^2}{1.2} + \chi''''(y)\frac{a^4x^4}{1.2.3.4} - \&c.$$

$$-\omega'(y)\frac{ax}{1} + \omega'''(y)\frac{a^3x^3}{1.2.3} - \&c.$$

which, as will be found on trial, satisfies the equation. A solution by series, however, can rarely be considered as quite sufficient.

52. In considering the motion of ordinary small waves in a sea of uniform depth (x horizontal in the direction in which the wave is going, y vertical measured upwards from the bottom), we find (see *Tides and Waves*)

$$\frac{d^2X}{dy^2} + \frac{d^2X}{dx^2} = 0.$$

The cumbrous form of the general solution of this equation would make it almost useless to attempt to apply it to the special case. But the nature of the case permits us to assume

$$X = R \cos (nt - mx) + S \sin (nt - mx),$$

where R and S are functions of y. Substituting, we have

$$\frac{d^2 R}{dy^2} - m^2 R = 0, \qquad \frac{d^2 S}{dy^2} - m^2 S = 0 ;$$

whence

$$R = C \epsilon^{my} + D \epsilon^{-my}, \qquad S = C' \epsilon^{my} + D' \epsilon^{-my} ;$$

and, after some reductions peculiar to the problem,

$$X = A \left(\epsilon^{my} + \epsilon^{-my} \right) \cos (nt - mx - B).$$

FINAL DETERMINATION OF THE FUNCTIONS WHICH ARE UNDETERMINED IN THE GENERAL SOLUTION.

53. In nearly the whole of these solutions, our resulting expression for the quantity which it is our object to find is accompanied with undetermined functions. It is now an object of great importance to determine those functions. Although in reality the process for doing this may be stated in brief rules, yet it will be better understood from an exhibition of its application in one or two actual instances than in any other way.

54. Example 1. In the consideration of the tidal motions of water without friction in an equatoreal channel round the earth, X being the horizontal displacement at

any time t of a particle whose ordinate measured round the channel from a fixed origin was x, the equation is

$$\frac{d^2X}{dt^2} = H\sin{(it-mx)}+c^2\frac{d^2X}{dx^2}\,;$$

where it is double the moon's hour-angle from the origin, and mx is double the longitude-angle of the point x from the same origin; and where c^2 is a constant depending on the depth of the water. This equation can be completely solved: its result is

$$X=\frac{H}{c^2m^2-i^2}\sin{(it-mx)}+\phi\,(ct+x)+\psi\,(ct-x)\,;$$

which we shall write

$$C\sin{(it-mx)}+\phi\,(ct+x)+\psi\,(ct-x).$$

Each of the three terms represents a wave, but they are waves of different characters. The first wave corresponds in its velocity with the lunar force $H\sin{(it-mx)}$ which produces it: for this the author has introduced the term *forced wave*; it depends entirely on the lunar force, and would not exist if there were no lunar force. The second wave is travelling in the direction opposite to the moon's apparent diurnal motion, and the third wave in the same direction as the moon's apparent diurnal motion; for these the author has introduced the term *free waves;* their velocity is independent of the moon's motion; the two waves, or either of them, may or may not exist; they are entirely independent of the moon's action, and the question of their existence is generally independent of the moon's action and of the forced wave. This is the state of things when there is no material limit to the length of the canal.

55.   But suppose that the canal is limited by the obstacle of land at its two ends (as in the Mediterranean Sea, all minor gulfs, &c., being put out of consideration). Then the forced wave alone is not sufficient for a solution.   For, the existence of the terminal obstacles (whose ordinates we will call a and b) requires that, at those obstacles, the horizontal displacement of the water be nothing at all times; and therefore when $x = a$ or $x = b$, X must $= 0$ whatever be the value of t.

Now this cannot hold with the forced wave alone; for, the values which the first term assumes for $x = a$ and $x = b$, namely, $C \sin (it - ma)$ and $C \sin (it - mb)$, will not vanish for all values of t. We must therefore have recourse to the two undetermined functions; or, in other words, we must now necessarily introduce the two free waves as an indispensable part of the solution: and we must determine their elements so that the two conditions, of X always $= 0$ when $x = a$ and when $x = b$, shall be satisfied.

56.   The term expressing the forced wave is a simple periodical term having it in its argument. Therefore, in order to destroy this at all times for definite values of x, the free waves must be expressed by simple periodical terms having it in their arguments. Therefore the two

undetermined terms $\phi\,(ct+x)$ and $\psi\,(ct-x)$ must have the forms

$$A_1 \sin\left\{\frac{i}{c}\,(ct+x)\right\} + B_1 \cos\left\{\frac{i}{c}\,(ct+x)\right\},$$

and

$$A_2 \sin\left\{\frac{i}{c}\,(ct-x)\right\} + B_2 \cos\left\{\frac{i}{c}\,(ct-x)\right\};$$

and the entire expression for X will have the form

$$C \sin (it - mx)$$

$$\perp A_1 \sin \left(it + \frac{i}{c}\,x\right) + B_1 \cos \left(it + \frac{i}{c}\,x\right)$$

$$+ A_2 \sin \left(it - \frac{i}{c}\,x\right) + B_2 \cos \left(it - \frac{i}{c}\,x\right);$$

or, expanding the trigonometrical terms, and putting e for $A_1 + A_2,$ f for $A_1 - A_2,$ g for $B_1 + B_2,$ h for $B_2 - B_1,$

$$X = \left\{ \begin{aligned} &\sin it \times \left\{ C \cos mx + e \cos \frac{ix}{c} + h \sin \frac{ix}{c} \right\} \\ &+ \cos it \times \left\{ - C \sin mx + f \sin \frac{ix}{c} + g \cos \frac{ix}{c} \right\}. \end{aligned} \right.$$

Making this $= 0$ when $x = a$ and when $x = b,$ and writing α for $\dfrac{ia}{c}$ and β for $\dfrac{ib}{c},$ we have the four equations,

$$0 = C \cos ma + e \cos \alpha + h \sin \alpha,$$

$$0 = - C \sin ma + f \sin \alpha + g \cos \alpha,$$

displacement of any point (see *Sound*, Article 73), the equation for z is

$$\frac{d^2z}{dt^2} - a^2 \frac{d^2z}{dx^2} = 0;$$

where $a^2 = gL$, L being that length of the same string whose weight will represent the tension of the string : and its solution is

$$z = \phi\,(at + x) + \psi\,(at - x).$$

Here the solution is expressed entirely by the two undetermined functions. If the initial circumstances of disturbance (namely, the displacement and the velocity of every point) were given, those functions could be determined, as will be shewn below. But even without an absolute knowledge of the forms of the functions, some very important properties of the solution may be ascertained thus.

58. Let the ordinate of the near end of the string be 0, and that of the further end l. Then, whatever be the value of t, z is 0 when $x = 0$ or when $x = l$. That is,

$$\phi\,(at) + \psi\,(at) = 0,$$

$$\phi\,(at + l) + \psi\,(at - l) = 0.$$

The first equation shews that ψ must always $= -\phi$. Thus one of the undetermined functions is already eliminated (the other will be eliminated from consideration of the initial circumstances).

Substituting in the second equation,

$$\phi\,(at + l) - \phi\,(at - l) = 0.$$

Now at may, with changes of time, receive any value

whatever. And if $at - l = q$ (which makes $at + l = q + 2l$), q may have any value whatever. And thus, q having any value whatever, we always have the equation

$$\phi(q + 2l) = \phi(q);$$

that is, the form of the function ϕ must be such that, on increasing or diminishing the quantity under the bracket by $2l$, the same value of the function will be reproduced. Now in either term of the expression for the displacement of the particle at x, namely

$$\phi(at + x) - \phi(at - x),$$

the increase by $2l$ of the quantity under the bracket may be effected by increasing at by $2l$, or by increasing t by $\dfrac{2l}{a}$.

Therefore, every time that we increase t by $\dfrac{2l}{a}$, we find the particle x with the same displacement as before. And this applies to every particle of the string. Consequently the string performs a complete vibration, returning again to the same position, in the time $\dfrac{2l}{a}$.

It is true that, as will shortly be seen, under certain circumstances the string may perform two or more complete vibrations in the same time, but it always returns to the same state after the interval $\dfrac{2l}{a}$; and this is the only interval of which it can be asserted that a return to the same state necessarily occurs in that time.

The reader may exercise his ingenuity in proving that the motion of the string consists in the simultaneous movements of two waves in opposite directions, each of which travels backwards and forwards from end to end with velocity a, and is reflected at each end.

59.   Putting, for the moment, θ for the quantity affected by the functional symbol ϕ, it appears that $\phi(\theta)$ is a finite periodical function, going through its changes and returning to the same value when θ is changed by $2l$. A trigonometric function of sines and cosines of an angle goes through all its changes and returns to the same value when the angle is increased by 2π.   Hence it appears that $\phi(\theta)$ is similar in its general character to a trigonometric function of sines and cosines of $\dfrac{2\pi \times \theta}{2l}$, or $\dfrac{\pi}{l}\theta$.   Any finite periodical magnitude may be represented with any assigned degree of approximation by a series of integral powers and combinations of the sine and cosine of $\dfrac{\pi}{l}\theta$; and these powers may be converted into sines and cosines of multiple arcs.   Thus the function $\phi(\theta)$ may be represented by

$$A_1 \sin\frac{\pi}{l}\theta + A_2 \sin\frac{2\pi}{l}\theta + \&\text{c.} + A_n \sin\frac{n\pi}{l}\theta + \&\text{c.}$$

$$+ B_1 \cos\frac{\pi}{l}\theta + B_2 \cos\frac{2\pi}{l}\theta + \&\text{c.} + B_n \cos\frac{n\pi}{l}\theta + \&\text{c.};$$

which may be conveniently expressed by

$$\Sigma\left(A_n \sin\frac{n\pi}{l}\theta\right) + \Sigma\left(B_n \cos\frac{n\pi}{l}\theta\right);$$

and thus the value of z will be

$$\Sigma \left\{ A_n \sin \frac{n\pi\,(at+x)}{l} \right\} + \Sigma \left\{ B_n \cos \frac{n\pi\,(at+x)}{l} \right\}$$

$$-\Sigma \left\{ A_n \sin \frac{n\pi\,(at-x)}{l} \right\} - \Sigma \left\{ B_n \cos \frac{n\pi\,(at-x)}{l} \right\},$$

or

$$\Sigma \left(2A_n \cos \frac{n\pi at}{l} \sin \frac{n\pi}{l} x \right)$$

$$-\Sigma \left(2B_n \sin \frac{n\pi at}{l} \sin \frac{n\pi}{l} x \right);$$

and the value of $\dfrac{dz}{dt}$ will be

$$-\Sigma' \left(\frac{2n\pi a}{l} A_n \sin \frac{n\pi at}{l} \sin \frac{n\pi}{l} x \right)$$

$$-\Sigma \left(\frac{2n\pi a}{l} B_n \cos \frac{n\pi at}{l} \sin \frac{n\pi}{l} x \right).$$

60. Suppose now that the initial circumstances of displacement (Z) and velocity (Z') are given for every point of the string, and that from these we desire to determine all the subsequent motions. We must now make $t = 0$, and we have

$$Z = \Sigma \left(2A_n \sin \frac{n\pi}{l} x \right), \qquad Z' = -\Sigma \left(\frac{2\pi a}{l} n B_n \sin \frac{n\pi}{l} x \right).$$

And our immediate object is, knowing the values of Z and Z' for every value of x, to determine the values of A_1, A_2, &c., B_1, B_2, &c.   This will be done by means of the following general formula.   If we multiply $\sin \frac{n\pi}{l} x$ by $\sin \frac{m\pi}{l} x$, where m is any integer different from n, and integrate from $x = 0$ to $x = l$, we have for product,

$$\frac{1}{2} \cos \frac{(m-n)\pi}{l} x - \frac{1}{2} \cos \frac{(m+n)\pi}{l} x;$$

for general integral,

$$\frac{l}{2(m-n)\pi} \sin \frac{(m-n)\pi}{l} x - \frac{l}{2(m+n)\pi} \sin \frac{(m+n)\pi}{l} x;$$

and for definite integral, 0.

But if $m = n$, we have for product

$$\frac{1}{2} - \frac{1}{2} \cos \frac{2n\pi}{l} x,$$

for general integral

$$\frac{x}{2} - \frac{l}{4n\pi} \sin \frac{2n\pi}{l} x,$$

and for definite integral, $\frac{l}{2}$.

Hence, if we put S for the integral with respect to x taken from $x = 0$ to $x = l$,

$$S\left(Z \sin \frac{n\pi}{l} x\right) = A_1 \, l;$$

$$S\left(Z \sin \frac{2n\pi}{l} x\right) = A_2 \, l, \text{ \&c.}$$

$$S\left(Z' \sin \frac{n\pi}{l} x\right) = -\pi an \, B_1;$$

$$S\left(Z' \sin \frac{2n\pi}{l} x\right) = -\pi an \, B_2, \text{ \&c.}$$

61. In a given instance, in which the initial displacements and velocities are given not by formula but by numerical values, the following process will apply. Suppose we limit the multiples of $\frac{\pi}{l} \theta$, where sines and cosines are to be used, to the first six, namely,

$$\frac{\pi}{l} \theta, \quad \frac{2\pi}{l} \theta, \quad \frac{3\pi}{l} \theta, \quad \frac{4\pi}{l} \theta, \quad \frac{5\pi}{l} \theta, \quad \frac{6\pi}{l} \theta,$$

which will suffice in almost any conceivable case. Divide the length l into 120 equal parts, and suppose that Z and Z' are known numerically for the middle of each of these parts.   For the first of these middles, $\dfrac{n\pi}{l}\,x = 45'$; for the second it is $3 \times 45'$; for the third it is $5 \times 45'$; and so on. And for each of these parts, the integral is, in fact, taken through the extent $\dfrac{l}{120}$.   Hence, the formula above gives the following numerical rule :—

Multiply the successive values of Z by $\sin 45'$, $\sin 3 \times 45'$, $\sin 5 \times 45'$, &c.: the sum of products $= 120\,A_1$.

Multiply the successive values of Z by $\sin 2 \times 45'$, $\sin 6 \times 45'$, $\sin 10 \times 45'$, &c.: the sum of products $= 120\,A_2$.

Multiply the successive values of Z by $\sin 3 \times 45'$, $\sin 9 \times 45'$, $\sin 15 \times 45'$, &c.: the sum of products $= 120\,A_3$.

And so to A_6.

And a similar process (with proper changes) determines B_1, B_2, &c., from the given values of Z'.

Then substituting these in the formulæ at the end of Article 59, the circumstances of all subsequent motion are completely obtained.

62.   If A_1, or B_1, or both, are found to have real values, and A_2, A_3, &c., B_2, B_3, &c., have no real values, then the vibration is that of a simple line of sines, de-

pending, for time, on the angle $\frac{\pi a t}{l}$. If only A_2 and B_2, one or both, have real values, then the vibration is that of two lines of sines; separated at the point where $\frac{2\pi}{l} x = \pi$, or where $x = \frac{l}{2}$, thus forming a permanent node in the middle of the length; and depending for time on the angle $\frac{2\pi a t}{l}$, and thus vibrating in half the time of the former vibration. Similarly if A_3 and B_3 only have real values, the string is divided into three equal parts by two nodes, and the vibrations are made in one-third of the time of the fundamental vibrations.

The connexion, of these results, with the results of the experience of the senses as to the musical tones produced, is one of the most important points in the Acoustical Theory of Music.

63. The two instances which we have given will probably suffice, better than any rules, to shew the use that is to be made of the undetermined functions in the solution of a Partial Differential Equation. For important applications, in the Theories of the simple Echo and of Resonance, see *Sound*, Articles 41 and 81.

CONSIDERATIONS ON THE NECESSITY OF CONNEXION BETWEEN THE NUMBER OF UNDETERMINED CONSTANTS AND THE ORDER OF THE EQUATION (IN SIMPLE DIFFERENTIAL EQUATIONS), AND BETWEEN THE NUMBER OF UNDETERMINED FUNCTIONS AND THE ORDER OF THE EQUATION (IN PARTIAL DIFFERENTIAL EQUATIONS).

64. In solving a simple differential equation of the first order, we usually arrive at a solution containing one undetermined constant. But it is not always so. There is a remarkable class of solutions called " particular solutions," which not only have not, but which cannot have, an undetermined constant. Thus, if we express in algebraical language the problem " To find the equation to the curve whose tangents possess this property, that a perpendicular from a given point upon the tangent has a given value;" we have, for general solution, a straight line with one undetermined constant; and for particular solution, a certain circle, which from the nature of the case does not admit an undetermined constant. The connexion, therefore, between the order of the equation and the number of undetermined constants in its solution is not invariable.

65. But if we assume a formula as solution to a differential equation which we propose to form, the said formula containing symbolical constants, we can predetermine that any one of those constants (if the equation be of the first order), or any two of those constants (if the

equation be of the second order), shall be eliminated from the differential equation to be formed, and shall therefore be undetermined when that equation is solved. Thus, to take a very simple instance, let $y = ax + b$ be assumed to be the solution of a differential equation, with the constant a undetermined. Differentiating it, $\dfrac{dy}{dx} = a$; substituting this in the given equation, $y - x\dfrac{dy}{dx} - b = 0$, the differential equation required. This process evidently can be extended to equations of any order.

66. It appears thus that the existence of a soluble differential equation does not necessarily imply an undetermined constant in the solution; but the existence or assumption of an undetermined constant in a solution can always be represented by proper form of a differential equation: and that this theorem applies to equations of every order.

67. If now we apply similar considerations to Partial Differential Equations, we are led to the following conclusions.

68. First, on examining the solution in Article 18, &c., it will be seen that, in the cases in which the solution of a Partial Differential Equation is really effected, it has been done by reducing it to an ordinary integration, just as would be done for a Simple Differential Equation. This

seems to indicate a probability that there may be cases in which the solution of a Partial Differential Equation has limitations analogous to those of a Simple Differential Equation, and therefore has not, and cannot have, an undetermined function in its solution. Upon this, however, there is not at present any distinct evidence, and the matter is indicated as one which appears to merit examination.

69. Second, if we assume a formula containing one function $\phi(w)$, where w is a definite function of x and y, and where ϕ is intended to be undetermined, we can always produce a Partial Differential Equation of the first order, of which the assumed formula will be the solution.

For we have

$$z, \text{ which contains } \phi(w);$$

and we can form

$$\frac{dz}{dx}, \text{ which will contain } \phi(w) \text{ and } \phi'(w);$$

$$\frac{dz}{dy}, \text{ which will contain } \phi(w) \text{ and } \phi'(w);$$

and from these three equations we can eliminate $\phi(w)$ and $\phi'(w)$, leaving .one equation· between z, x, y, $\dfrac{dz}{dx}$, and $\dfrac{dz}{dy}$, of the form required.

D. E.   F

70.   But, third, if we assume a formula containing two functions $\phi(w)$ and $\psi(s)$, where w and s are definite functions of x and y, and where ϕ and ψ are intended to be undetermined, we cannot always produce a Partial Differential Equation of the second order, of which the assumed formula will be the solution. For, we have

$$z, \text{ which contains } \phi(w) \text{ and } \psi(s);$$

and we can form

$$\frac{dz}{dx}, \text{ which will contain } \phi(w), \phi'(w), \psi(s), \psi'(s);$$

$$\frac{dz}{dy}, \text{ which will contain } \phi(w), \phi'(w), \psi(s), \psi'(s);$$

$$\frac{d^2z}{dx^2}, \text{ which will contain } \phi(w), \phi'(w), \phi''(w), \psi(s),$$

$$\psi'(s), \psi''(s);$$

$$\frac{d^2z}{dxdy}, \text{ which will contain the same six functions};$$

$$\frac{d^2z}{dy^2}, \text{ which will contain the same six functions.}$$

Here we have six equations, and no more, with six functions on the other side of the equations. We cannot therefore eliminate these six functions, so as to leave an equation between

$$z,\ x,\ y,\ \frac{dz}{dx},\ \frac{dz}{dy},\ \frac{d^2z}{dx^2},\ \frac{d^2z}{dxdy},\ \frac{d^2z}{dy^2}.$$

And thus we cannot always produce the Partial Differential Equation required. The same remark, it will be found, applies more strongly to equations of a higher order.

71. It seems not impossible that the failure of attempts to solve the equations in Article 44 may have some connexion with this inability to establish a perfect connexion between the order of the equation and the number of undetermined functions. The subject appears to be worthy of greater attention than it has received.

9 789391 270315

$$0 = C \cos mb + e \cos \beta + h \sin \beta,$$

$$0 = - C \sin mb + f \sin \beta + g \cos \beta.$$

Solving these equations,

$$e \sin (\beta - \alpha) = C (- \cos ma . \sin \beta + \cos mb . \sin \alpha),$$

$$f \sin (\beta - \alpha) = C (- \sin ma . \cos \beta + \sin mb . \cos \alpha),$$

$$g \sin (\beta - \alpha) = C (\sin ma . \sin \beta - \sin mb . \sin \alpha),$$

$$h \sin (\beta - \alpha) = C (\cos ma . \cos \beta - \cos mb . \cos \alpha).$$

Substituting, and restoring the original notation,

$$X = \frac{H}{c^2 m^2 - i^2} \sin (it - mx) - \frac{H}{(c^2 m^2 - i^2) \sin \left\{ \frac{i}{c} (b - a) \right\}} \times$$

$$\left[\sin (it - ma) . \sin \left\{ \frac{i}{c} (b - x) \right\} + \sin (it - mb) . \sin \left\{ \frac{i}{c} (x - a) \right\} \right].$$

Thus the terms, undetermined in the general solution, are now completely determined so as to satisfy the special conditions of the problem.   The entire expression for X, it will be seen, satisfies the original partial differential equation, and also makes $X = 0$ at all times when $X = a$ and $x = b$.

57.   Example 2.   In the ordinary problem of vibrating musical strings, where no force is supposed to act after the string has been put in motion, x being measured longitudinally along the string and z being the small transversal